Mairhi Rowes

B U R N I N G   L O V E

I0456957

MAIRHI ROWES

# Burning love

*Stranger at the funeral*

2023

# Contents

# Burning love

What was he doing here. Laura would have known him anywhere., tall, sparkling blue eyes curly hair now tinged with grey, the sapling of a youth now a man. The same electric shock as our eyes met. Laura was remembering that moment 40 years ago when she knew she had met her soul mate Blake. She had to block all that out, more friends were streaming in after all it was George's funeral and she and George had known many of them most all their lives. She needed to accept the condolences being offered and was so thankful for the support of her four children, Nicholas, Thomas and twin daughters Kate and Helen. I Laura hoped people just put her dazed state down to being shock over George's sudden death. The wake seemed to go on forever and she was glad when she could go home and put her feet up. She mused over Blake, was he really there, thinking back to when we were 19 years old, the magic of our first kiss when the sun the moon and the stars were all bursting around them, knowing something wonderful had happened and existed between them. Laura now continues, remembering and thinking how hot we were for each other, how he would run his hands down my sides and pull me hard against him, both knowing we wanted to share more of each other, not just kisses hot and passionate as they were.

Exhaustion finally took over and I fell asleep only to dream of Blake. Next day I was still thinking, did I imagine Blake's appearance, was he really there, or had it all been a figment of my imagination. My children and family friends were calling in to see if I was okay, kind of them and to be expected, however I was still vague and spaced out. They didn't know I was remembering my teenage lover who had always held a place in my heart, nor that seeing him had awakened memories I had stored away in a corner of my heart never to be forgotten.

Now my brief glance had taken in a handsome, distinguished businessman who made me burning hot with desire. Really, my thoughts were disgusting but George and I had not shared a bed for over 10 years and although I cooked his meals, he often just stayed at the 19th hole of the golf club. Exhaustion finally took over and I went to sleep in my recliner chair. Next day I was still thinking did I imagine Blake's appearance, was he really there. It was 6 months later before I had any answers.

In the next six months whilst I was dealing with George's Will and disposing of his possessions, my thoughts were often drifting back to Blake and the past and what might have been, how red hot we were for each other how we couldn't keep our hands of each other, how he would pull me into his arms, hold me so tight like he'd never let me, the magic of his kisses our longing for more of each other. I knew how great we would have been together. These memories, so vivid, brought back by his unexpected appearance at Geoge's funeral..

# George's Will

George's will was simple enough as during his lifetime George had transferred the Vineyard and Winery to Thomas, and the broadacre farm to Nicholas along with the cattle and commercial flock of sheep. The boys had been managing their respective farms for years with help from George whenever they needed it. George and I, did most of the work at "Home Farm" my farm, given to me by my father when I married George. (I imagine it eased his conscience for the bombastic and domineering way he had virtually forced me to marry George). I had also been given a stud merino flock which we had expanded. I always did all the recording of the progeny, each ewe and the ram had to be recorded I was hoping grandson Dale would take that over as he seemed interested in the stud and all it entailed. Nicholas sowed all the crops, cut the hay, and reaped the grain most of this was for his sheep and cattle and the stud on the 'home farm.' Our twin girls, Kate, and Helen, inherited a generous Legacy, which George had set up many years ago. George had also set up an investment trust which I was to receive the income from during my lifetime. All four children had the opportunity to take whatever of George's possessions they wanted. I am not proud of this but whilst my hands were busy sorting out clothes for donating to the Salvation Army, and other personal possessions for the children.to take their pick. I couldn't get Blake out of my thoughts as I kept wondering how and why he had appeared at George's funeral. There were so many questions with no answers.

I continued to keep busy outside with my garden, going to the Gym, and soon Tennis would be starting. I enjoyed all these activities, and they helped me keep fit and trim. Neighbours and friends continued to call in to see if I was coping with life without George, even though most of them knew he spent most of his time at the 19th hole of the Golf club. Loneliness was not an issue as I was used to spending my time at home and in the garden, when not playing sport. My friends and I often enjoyed a coffee and chat after a gym session.

# No Holiday Yet

The family kept pressing me to go on a holiday and have a good break. I would do this when I wanted to, for now there was plenty to see to in the garden and I needed to teach grandson Dale more about the stud. I needed to decide where I would go and with whom. My thoughts would often stray to Blake and what might have been. I just could not get Blake out of my mind; imagining how hot and excited he made me feel, and how we longed to be together. His appearance at George's funeral had awakened all those old memories of the love we shared, which was denied to us by my domineering father.

# Soul Mates Met

I will never forget the wet night when we had been playing Table Tennis in the Gym and Blake had been coaching me. I guess we flirted a bit, but it was what happened afterwards that is etched in my mind never to go away. It was raining when we went outside to go home. I offered Blake a ride as he had walked to the Gym, and I had driven in my father's car. As we got into the car, we turned at the same time to put our bats on the back seat and our lips met, involuntarily my mouth opened under his lips and there it was the sun, the moon and stars were bursting around us. We both knew something out of this world had happened. We had met our soul mates. Trembling I started the car and drove Blake the short distance to his boarding house. We didn't want to part, he held me tight, his arms so strong as his kisses rained upon my quivering mouth. Neither of us spoke as we linked hands not wanting to part but knowing we must.

Next day Blake rang me at my workplace and arranged to see me after work. I was in a state of excitement and couldn't concentrate on anything. Would the day never end, I kept glancing at the clock until at last it was

5.00pm. My stomach was churning, and I felt hot with excitement as I walked out of the door to where Blake was waiting. I wanted to rush into his arms but knew I mustn't in the view of the prying eyes of my work mates who had during the day asked me why I was in such a twitter.

Blake took my hand, and we started walking to my home, we went the back way down over the wooden swing bridge at Dead man's pass. Blake was curious about this name. I explained that a dead man was found in a tree there, probably to escape the flood waters of the South Para River. In a very wet season torrents of water would come rushing down from the hills and the river would flood and even reach the height of the main bridge into Gawler, "The Mill Inn Bridge." A flour mill was on the riverbank adjacent to the bridge, hence the name. I told Blake how rode my bike across this bridge each day on my way to Gawler Primary School. Morton Bay Fig trees grew on the banks of the river there and provided welcome shade on hot days.

We stopped occasionally for a cuddle and a kiss, on and up the hill (Riggs), also known as Lovers Lane, Couples often parked up there after a dance or pictures in Gawler. My father had built a modern and ostentatious house at the foot of the hill, when he leased his farms after an accident which had caused severe injury to his left leg. Blake was over-awed he told me his Grand-mother and Grandfather had reared him, on their family farm at Mount Pleasant, after his parents and siblings were killed in a car accident when he was 9 years old. (He did not tell me that he would inherit a fortune when he was 25). I knew now why he always showed his respect for older people. My feelings for him were sorrow, respect, and love. We sat on the garden bench under the shade of a large gum tree and continued to talk. My father came home, and Blake felt the immediate tension and said he must go. He rang next day and invited me to go out with him, to his Football Club annual ball. I wanted to go and said I would meet him there, as my father had given me a lecture about his intention that I should marry George, and that I should not go on a giddy round-about of dating. I knew if Blake came to pick me up there would be a showdown. My feelings and what I wanted did not matter.

# Domineering Father

George and I had grown up like brother and sister as his parents and mine were great friends and of course they were pushing for us to get engaged and marry. We had been in the same group of friends since school days in Gawler. Some of us finished our education at different colleges in Adelaide which broadened our outlook on life and work options other than our hometown. My father decreed I should work in Gawler, so he could keep an eye on me I suppose. George was keen to continue escorting me to events with our old group of friends and I was happy enough. I told George I regarded him as a brother and loved him like a brother. He was well respected and a good fellow, but there was no fire in our relationship. I just didn't want to marry George. It would be a marriage of convenience. He was wealthy and could give me everything, but I knew I didn't love him, and I told him so.

Kissing George just felt like I was kissing a sibling, there was no spark in it for me, but I felt I owed it to George to tell him about Blake. George wasn't coming to the Annual Football Club Ball I told him I was going to go. I had been drifting along happy enough with

George taking me around. George wanted to become engaged, and I didn't but was getting pressured by my parents, especially my father. I was a romantic and kept wondering if there was any truth in the stories I heard. Where was the explosion, the sun the moon and the stars EXPLODING when he kissed me? And now I knew it did happen. It just didn't happen with George, there wasn't even a spark. I would just get out of the car, say see you later, and go inside.

Back in those days going steady meant seeing each other once a week or sometimes twice, going to a dance or the pictures, still living with your parents and certainly no hanky panky. A kiss or two and a cuddle, that was "goodnight." There were some girls who obviously did more than that because they got pregnant. My father was the do as I say type and mother was very strict, being well schooled on how to behave I was too scared of them to indulge in sex, and to be truthful George didn't inspire me to even feel that way inclined. I knew he was not my soul mate. It was so different when Blake and I kissed I just melted in his arms. I have no doubt, had my father not intervened, Blake and I would have found it very hard not to indulge in premarital sex.

# The Football Club Ball

I remember so well Blake's football club annual ball. The Ball was to be in the Gawler Institute Ball Room which was upstairs and had magnificent highly polished dancing floor. The Library and Municipal offices were underneath; it was the Civic centre of Gawler.

I will never forget that night, climbing the stairs, excitement and anticipation growing with each step as the romantic waltz played by the band floated down the stairs.

I wore an ice-white frock with nipped in waistline, full skirt and cross over bodice that was trimmed with guipure lace. The dress alone was stunning, but with my black curly hair, clear complexion, blue eyes and plus the exotic large white earrings, I knew I looked stunning. I walked into the Ballroom; would Blake be there waiting for me to arrive. I went over to group of friends and sat down. The Band was playing the haunting music for a slow foxtrot, the sounds were exciting and thrilling me and the longing to be in Blake's arms and dance was consuming me. I felt Blake's gaze upon me as our eyes locked the surge of emotion was instantaneous. Would he never come and ask me to dance! I was impatient to be in his arms. Other boys I knew were coming toward me, with lightning speed Blake cut in front of them took my hand and asked me to dance.

"Now I see it all, you take my breath away" he whispered as he took me in his arms. We were happy dancing, our steps matching perfectly but it was hard to talk over the band. Blake suggested we take a breather out on the balcony of the Institute. It was very romantic with the lights of the town twinkling all round us. He held me in his arms and kissed my throat and nuzzled my ears before seeking my mouth and the instant explosion of moon and stars bursting around us was breathtaking. A driver honking his car's horn as he drove along Murray Street, (the main street of Gawler) brought us back to reality.

We had the balcony to ourselves and talked about his football career, he had been approached by Port Adelaide to play in the Adelaide competition. I knew I would miss seeing him and said so, but congratulated him on this achievement. He asked me about George and what he meant to me as he had seen me out with him and our group of friends often. Well, I could truthfully say, George was like the brother I never had and that our parents were lifelong friends, we grew up almost like brother and sister and that I regarded him as a brother and nothing more.

We returned to the ballroom, and danced as one for the rest of the night. Blake walked me home, hand in hand chatting, totally at ease with each other. From the moment our lips met I knew I had met my soul mate and all I wanted was to be in his arms and be with him. I wondered did he feel the same. I felt sure he did. The desire and electricity between us so beautiful, so dynamic becoming more intense with each kiss. My body would meld to his as desire mounted and the want for more than kisses consumed us both.

## We couldn't Elope

**B**lake rang me many times, and I always knew it was him before I picked up the 'phone. Blake often came to see me at home, but my father always sent him packing. I had told George I would not marry him, but George was being very difficult saying "Blake was just a flash in the pan." Blake and I would sit on the front step of the veranda planning our future but when my father came home Blake was ordered off the place. I was given another lecture by my father then two days later Blake was transferred from his position in the Savings Bank in my hometown to a position in the city, end of story, not quite. A week later he came to my home, I knew it was him before I opened the door. He had caught a train from Adelaide and walked from the Gawler train station to my home again. We sat on the front step of the veranda and talked, he told me he only had his wage each week and didn't have much else to offer at the present time. I never questioned him I was just happy he wanted me as much as I wanted him. The magic of our being together was so strong I just didn't want the night to end. WE discussed eloping, as neither of us owned a car so we couldn't elope, we needed to come up with another plan.

Then my father came home, ordered me to go inside and told Blake to go and don't come back again. After Blake had gone my father again said "you are not to see him again. you have a reliable, steady boyfriend who wants to marry you, who can give you everything and who has my blessing." What I wanted didn't matter, that was obvious. He didn't even bother to find out anything about Blake's life and the sadness he had experienced losing his parents and siblings in a car cash when he was nine years old. That Blake would inherit a large fortune when he was 25 years from his late parents' estate, and which had been invested in a trust fund administered by his Grandparents. I did not know it at that time and even if I had it wouldn't have changed my feelings, I loved Blake for himself and his honesty.

# No Say at all

Blake's friend Colin who I often saw, told me that my father who banked at the Savings bank and was a friend of the bank manager had evidently been in and then bingo Blake was transferred again this time to Sydney head office of the National Bank, where after further training, he became a relieving Bank Manager and was constantly on the move all over branches in the Sydney suburbs and then in country areas. I know now that he wrote to me often, but I never received the letters, which of course was my father's doing. Sometimes I thought my mother looked guilty when I asked if there was any mail for me, but she would not have gone against my father's orders. It wasn't until after she died that among her possessions I found a locked storage box, which I put in our attic to open and look in at some future time. Years later when I did open the storage box, I was so sad, angry, and hurt that I had been cheated by the withholding of my mail. Blake's love for me jumped out of the pages and I cried until had no tears left. No doubt my father's orders and my mother would not have defied him. My father's domineering influence over me was very strong and I let his words rule me, I had never defied him.

I always regretted not defying him to follow my heart, and seek Blake out through Colin who kept in touch with him. Colin was being transferred to Melbourne and so I would no longer see him and losing contact with him meant no news of Blake. My father announced in the local paper," Laura Shannon and George Angas are engaged and will marry on 8th March 1974", I had no say in it at all, I regretted not defying my father all my life. Blake was tucked away in a corner of my heart. The place my thoughts went to when life felt unbearable. I knew he was my soul mate. In the modern world of today I would have run away and through his work, found Blake. Now here he was 40 years later at George's funeral. What did it mean?

I was watching the Crows and Geelong in an AFL match. The half time siren had just sounded when the 'phone rang; my had trembled as I reached to pick it up, I knew instinctively that it was Blake. He told me he had waited six months out of respect for George. He was not to know that George and I had virtually lived our own lives for over 10 years and did not share a bed or a bedroom by mutual agreement.

Blake is a Geelong fan and I a very ardent Crow, so we had quite a discussion on the football, the siren sounded, to restart the game, and Blake asked could he ring me again. I had enjoyed talking with him so much I said "I'd like that" I could feel the electricity between us even then, I know it was not my imagination. I wondered if he felt it too.

The following Friday Blake rang again the same electrifying connection seemed to float down the wire. This time we talked for an hour or more the time seemed to fly, comparing the events of the last week. We had a common interest in politics and the state of the nation. He made me feel so happy and said he would ring again. Soon we were talking twice a week. Our lives and interests paralleled in so many ways. More than ever, I felt we were made for each other.

We talked about our respective families. His wife, Grace, had died five years ago. They a had twin sons Philip and Edward and two daughters, Kirsty, and Camille. Phillip died as the result of a car accident when he was 18. Grace never came to terms with her grief and her health declined. Blake cared for her until her death.

Edward and the girls, Kirsty, and Camille, were all married, each with three children. Blake was grooming Edward to take over the management of the family business and the girl's husbands were also involved one as a marketing manager and the other as buyer for The Jackson Corporation, importers of fine diamonds and makers of unique designer jewelry, sought after world-wide. My curiosity was well and truly aroused, but I would wait for him to tell me how he came to be Managing Director of this prestigious firm.

# Our Families

After Blake was transferred to Sydney head office, he had further training, for a fortnight then put on the relieving Management staff and never knew where he would be next, he became sick of living out of a suitcase and never being in any town long enough to become involved in sport and other activities. He decided to look out for some other position and answered an advertisement for a Financial Officer with the Jackson Corporation. Colin had told him I was now married to George, and he stopped writing to me. I told Blake I never received any letters from him, another example of how determined my father was for me to marry George. Sometimes, when I asked if there was any mail for me, I thought my mother looked guilty (I now knew why) but she would never defy my father's instructions. We talked on and on, our hobbies, our sports, our friends, politics our pets and other interests we had so much in common. Hiking, tennis, and Bowls, my keen gardening pursuits and attending Gym.

It was my turn to tell Blake about my family of four children, sons Nicholas and Thomas both married and each with three children, twin girls Kate and Helen both married and each with two children. The girls lived in country South Australia, Kate at Kadina, and Helen at Clare, not far from my farm "Home Farm" at Angaston which Nicholas and Thomas now managed along with their own farms. Blake and I agreed our grandchildren added another dimension to our lives.

There was always the unasked question, about our previous marriages.

# Arranged Marriage

I told Blake how my father had insisted I become engaged and marry George. I was not consulted and *was married within six months.* I always had a feeling of guilt, (I don't know why, because it was my father who insisted on the marriage). I did get excited looking at wedding dresses and trying them on imagining I was walking down the aisle and marrying Blake, and I enjoyed helping the bridesmaids choose their dresses, they were so excited. The pre-wedding parties were good fun. If only I was marrying Blake, I thought so many times.

Walking down the aisle of the Chapel I did not feel excited, only regret that it was not Blake waiting at the altar for me. I repeated the wedding vows after the Pastor and wondered if I would be struck dead, but I did love Geroge (albeit LIKE A BROTHER). The guests were more excited than I was. George was a good person, and we had a marriage built on trust and friendship. The reception was very lavish, my father never did anything by halves. We dined and wined and the guests were happier than I was as I threw my bouquet high in the air, I didn't see who caught it I didn't care. I just hoped they got to marry the man they loved. George and I left in a limousine, our destination the airport: as generous George had booked our honeymoon in Italy. No expense was spared, and George saw to it that we visited all the notable sites. I submitted to my wifely duty and came home from our honeymoon pregnant; I was only 20. I tried hard to make the marriage a success and as our children were born in quick succession (4 children under 4) I never had time to brood, If I wasn't pushing in a bottle one end, I was changing a napkin the other. The marriage became tolerable. We pulled together to make the lives of our children the best we could. They meant the world to each of us and neither of us would have done anything to hurt or embarrass them. I was very busy with playgroup, kindergarten and preschool and as they got older, school canteen and parents club, and driving them to all their sports practices, dance classes and other hobbies at different venues took up a lot of my time. George usually went to the Golf club and didn't share the running around, even then he preferred staying at the 19th hole.

# Toleration

I enjoyed helping in the winery and working with the sheep stud and cattle on our farms. We were both very much involved in our community and enjoyed playing tennis and following the local football and netball teams in which the children played. George was a very keen golfer, I never liked the game as it seemed pointless to hit a little white ball as far as you could and them walk after it, although the exercise was good. In later years, our relationship deteriorated into one of toleration, and not always amicable. We agreed to stay together for the family. For over 10 years prior to his death we had separate rooms, but shared mealtimes and sometimes watched football together, but for the most part George stayed at the 19th hole of the Golf Club.

We did share an interest in AFL and in particular the Crows and that was about all. Our grandchildren added a new dimension to our lives, and we shared the joy as each and every one of them arrived. Life was more tolerable again with these young people.

# George is dead

George had gone to the Golf Club with his friend Bill on the day of his death. I was still out in the garden when I was surprised to hear Bill's car coming back just on "Dinner time" which was unusual. I sensed something was wrong; when there was no sign of George, then Bill told me George had collapsed and died on the fairway. He had called an ambulance before he came and told me what had happened. I was thankful George did not suffer a prolonged illness and had died doing what he loved.

# The Jackson Corporation

It was now Blake's turn to tell me more about his life with Grace which in some ways, I now knew, was very similar to mine. Sick of living out of a suitcase Blake had applied for the position of Financial Manager for the 'Jackson Corporation.' The owner Director of the Corporation (Walter Jackson) was Grace's father. Blake felt an immediate bond with Walter and was very pleased when he secured the position. On finding out that Blake didn't have a home, and was virtually living out of a suitcase, Walter offered him the use of the granny flat at their residence. Walter had been diagnosed with cancer and his health was rapidly deteriorating, he knew his lifetime was limited, he wanted Blake to start as soon as possible so Blake accepted this offer. Walter invited Blake to have dinner with the family every night so he and Blake could discuss the business and related matters afterwards. He offered Blake a Directorship which was a huge and generous offer. Walter had four daughters, he told Blake he was like the son he never had, he wanted to adopt Blake and for Blake to take the Jackson name. Blake told Walter how his mother, father and sisters were killed in a car accident when he was nine and his maternal grandparents, had cared for him until he finished his education at the Adelaide University graduating in Financial Management. Blake said he would only take the Jackson name for business purposes but still remain Blake Kaine for all other events in his personal life. Grace was also a director and she and Blake by necessity often attended meetings together. Blake knew Walter wanted him to court Grace as he had said he would die a happy man if Blake and Grace were to fall in love.

# Grace

Walter wanted to establish a branch of the Jackson Corporation in Melbourne, and offered Blake the opportunity to do so and be the Managing Director. This was an honour and a challenge which Blake accepted.

Blake told Grace he admired and respected her, but she was not his soul mate, and that his transfer to New South Wales from South Australia was engineered to break up his romance with another who was his soul mate and who held a place in his heart. They decided to marry and make the marriage work and together grew a very successful business. Like my life, as they had children it became more tolerable. His escape had been the business which he expanded and the Jackson Corporation, importers of fine diamonds and makers of unique designer jewelry, became well known world-wide, their unique jewelry much sought after. They had the sadness of losing their son, Philip, in a car accident, at which time he and Grace were united in their grief. Grace never coped with Phillips death and developed severe depression as this worsened Blake cared for her until her death. It seemed our lives paralleled in many ways.

# Thanks to the Japanese Buyers

I eventually asked Blake how he came to be at George's funeral. Fate played a hand in this. A group of Japanese jewelry buyers were coming over and asked Blake could they meet in Adelaide and have a trip to the Barossa Valley Wine region before going to Melbourne to select the jewelry they wanted to purchase. Blake arranged this and the buyers flew direct to Adelaide and Blake flew over from Melbourne. He was waiting for them at the airport and picked up an Advertiser which had been left on the seat beside him. He idly started perusing this and read the death notice of George Angas, husband of Laura, and the funeral arrangements. Surely it must be me, he thought or a huge coincidence. As the group would be at Seppeltsfield Winery that afternoon he arranged for the Japanese buyers to have lunch there and explained to them he would be coming back to pick them up a bit later. They were happy tasting wine and dining on the fine foods provided and jabbering away to each other in their own lingo.

The bus driver was willing to drive Blake over to Angaston. It was a short time frame but long enough he said to know I was still his soul mate. He had felt the tug at his heartstrings, and the chemistry between us, just as I had when our eyes met. I had never believed in fate but was beginning to wonder if maybe there was such a thing, and some things are meant to be. Was our destiny evolving?

# Phone Calls

We soon progressed from twice weekly 'phone calls to every night, never at a loss for words, always interested in the day's events and each other's families and their doings.

Every 'phone call the surging, burning flood of emotion powered through the phone lines, becoming more intense with each call. Both secretly knowing we wanted to meet, to be together, neither quite sure what the outcome would be or if the time was right. The pit of my stomach seemed to turn to jelly, and warmth encompassed me each time my trembling hand reached for the phone.

Blake was having 8 weeks leave as he felt it was time to see if Edward could manage the whole business without him. It was then he asked me if I would meet him so we could spend time together. I was very happy to say I would. Anticipation and excitement occupied my thoughts was this going to be a lovers' tryst or, dare I hope, a prelude to something more.

# Rendezvous

As Blake lived in his apartment in Melbourne and I lived in the Barossa Valley, SA, it was decided to meet in Adelaide. I left the arrangements to Blake. He soon rang to tell me he had booked a suite at the Stamford Grande at Glenelg for four weeks. Were we mad at our age? But I didn't feel old, I was that young 19 years old again and obviously Blake too, had turned back the hands of time. That flame ignited so long ago still burnt with intensity between us.

Our getting together may seem to some premature, we had known each other over 40 years ago and had talked constantly for six months, we both knew we wanted to be together and see where it went. Whether it was just physical or of greater depth.

It was for four weeks ahead so as to give us both time to put arrangements in place. Blake would fly over early on the Wednesday morning, and I would pick him up from the Airport. It seemed the four weeks would never end, even though I was busy deciding what to take and have my hair and nails done. I sure was glad that my body was in good shape thanks to the tennis, gym, and gardening.

I went to Adelaide on the Tuesday for some shopping, I needed some new after five frocks and evening wear, I also bought some frivolous night wear, was I mad! As it turned out I needn't have bothered about the nightwear as Blake said he preferred me naked so he could caress my velvety smooth skin. I had never slept in the raw before and found it was an exciting feeling so intimate, especially with our warm bodies touching, and available to each other.

# Holiday

The family had been urging me to have a break for ages so no questions were asked when I told them I would be away for a few weeks holiday with an old friend, they didn't even ask who, and I didn't tell them that my old friend was Blake. Grandson Dale, now 17, was more than keen to move into my house and look after my pet sheep "Bonnie and Clyde" my cat Freddie and Labrador Bella. I had been teaching him about the recording necessary for the stud, he was interested in that, and I hoped he would take it over now he was 17 and itching to leave home.

# At the Airport

It was time to head to the airport. My feeling of anticipation was growing, and excitement was mounting the closer I got to the airport then waiting for Blake's flight to land. It seemed an eternity, now it was landing. I was feeling nervous about how we would greet each other, my head was spinning, my stomach was turning cartwheels and I felt hot then cold, then I saw him walking up the gangway, so handsome and distinguished he stood out from other passengers. Our eyes met and it was like a charge of electricity shot through me, as his eyes held mine. I felt red hot with excitement and anticipation, my palms were sweaty, and my legs felt like jelly as was the pit of my stomach as he strode toward me. Soon he was right in front of me, he took me in his arms and held me close and kissed me with passion and intensity his wet lips sending shivers of excitement through the core of my body, a burning sensation of longing and want for more encompassed me as he held me to him in a long hug. I felt like I had come home. I felt sure my forehead would bear the mark of the red-hot kiss he bestowed there before we parted. We realized there were some interested onlookers. It was time to move on.

We chatted idly as hand in hand we made our way down to the luggage carousel. The usual banter about airline snacks etc. Soon his bags appeared, and we were able to load them on a trolley and make our way back to my car. He stowed his bags in the boot, then we headed off to Glenelg. I felt nervous driving when Blake was the passenger, I was in such a twitter, and it was good to arrive there. The concierge arranged for my car to be parked in the car park for guests, and the Bellhop attended to all our luggage. Blake attended to the signing in then we went to the lift. (I never asked how he signed in). Our luggage had already been delivered to our suite when we got up there.

# The Suite

It was a magnificent suite. Stepping in onto the plush carpet, so soft, I wanted to kick off my shoes. The room was beautifully appointed, a two -seater lounge and two chairs beside the fireplace, the burning logs were glowing and the aroma from them added ambience to the room. On a small table conveniently placed near the lounge was an Ice bucket complete with a bottle of champagne and two glittering crystal glasses.

The mantel piece above the fireplace had brass ornaments in various animal shapes upon it. The leopard with its foot on the neck of mongoose sent my imagination into overdrive as did the panther. Was I about to fall prey to the handsome sexy love of my life who had found me again. I felt sure Blake would be more subtle than that. The Grandfather clock's steady tick, tock each minute was it counting down to what was to come. The clock stood in one corner opposite an antique table above this hung an ornate gold mirror, reflections from the log fire danced in the mirror. An urn of beautiful red roses stood on the table, I wondered if Blake had organized them, and were there thirteen. A Chandelier was suspended from an ornate rose design in the centre of the room and the little lights glittered with the reflections from the burning logs. The rose design also featured in the cornices of the room. The plush carpet continued into the two bedrooms which opened off the lounge area and had a connecting door. The balcony extended from in front of the lounge across the front of the bedrooms. The main bedroom had a walk-in robe, a shoe rack, a dressing table, and lounge chair. The King size bed looked inviting with an embossed satin quilt and several scatter cushions. The red rose on one pillow made my heart beats quicken. Did Blake put it here!!

The suite was very luxurious. Each bedroom had its own amenities which we didn't really need, we were happy to share the amenities and it wasn't long before we did. The double doors which opened out from the lounge to the balcony looked out over the beach to the sea, a gentle sea breeze was wafting in. The sea looked so tranquil. A wicker table and two chairs were invitingly placed on the balcony. We were both eager to change into casual clothes and as it was past lunchtime Blake had ordered refreshments to be sent up to the suite via room service. It was a lovely sunny day, so we ate out on the balcony, it was so peaceful looking out over the beach, watching the waves roll in and the seagulls busy as always screeching when they found a crust. The cucumber sandwiches and fresh pineapple were delicious and very satisfying. We both loved the sea and decided to go for a walk along the beach. We were so at peace with each other, and conversation flowed freely as we walked. The sea was so tempting that we ran in and frolicked in the water like twitterpated teenagers playfully splashing each other. The water was cold and refreshing and soon we were getting cold. We ran along the beach to our towels which were lovely and warm as we rubbed ourselves dry. We paddled along the shore toward West Beach occasionally pausing on the edge, our feet sinking in the sand as the tide washed over them, like the sands of time I commented to Blake, his eyes held mine as he said, "Is it too late for us?." "I hope not" I whispered almost too moved to speak under his intense gaze, his arm resting on my shoulders tightened. We rested for a while watching the little sailing boats, their brilliant white sails bobbing along in the breeze as they headed back to the marina. The sun was sinking below the horizon, like a fire ball drowning in the sea. Dusk was fast falling as we paddled back, it was quite a way, and we were ready for a long cool drink, again we had this sent up to our suite. I must have dozed off and it was quite dark when I awakened to Blake's steady gaze. "Time to dress for Dinner" he said.

# The Blue Dress

The wind and salt water had played havoc with my hair, and it was a tangled mess, I showered and shampooed my hair and felt refreshed. It was hard to control my unruly curls, I took care with my makeup. I wanted to look my best. I was glad I had bought the cobalt blue silk dress, with a wide portrait neckline and the side seam which opened to the thigh, it was modest yet sexy. I knew I looked good in it and felt confident as I walked back into the lounge. Blake was standing by the balcony door, and I thought how handsome and distinguished he looked in his charcoal grey suite, white shirt and blue tie. He heard me come into the room and turned, our eyes locked and a feeling of warmth for him engulfed me. I knew I desired him and his love. "You take my breath away you look stunning' Blake said. "Do you remember the first time you said that to me"? "I've never forgotten that night" he answered. "Nor I," I managed to whisper in a wavery voice "You look pretty spiff yourself." The Grandfather clock and the town clock simultaneously striking seven brought us back to the present which was just as well as desire was raging through us. Blake said, "I booked our table for 7.00pm we better go down now". We were careful not to get too close to each other in the lift as we both secretly knew that would be the end of going down to dinner, such was the electricity and want surging between us. Blake had booked a table for two, in a quiet secluded corner of the dining room. The Head waiter greeted us and led us to our table. It was candlelit, this added to the romantic atmosphere. He drew out our chairs, saw us seated and with a flourish put a napkin on each of our laps, and said our orders would be taken shortly. The wine waiter was hovering Blake said, "tonight calls for Champagne don't you think," I could only nod in agreement. The waiter returned with the bottle and poured some into my glass first for my approval, before filling my glass he then filled Blakes. Blake said "A toast to old friends and new beginnings" our eyes locked a we clinked glasses. Sipping the bubbly, the tingling in my mouth was matched by fire in my veins and as we drank, the last of my inhibitions were fading away. I knew I wanted him above all else. We gazed at each other and talked trivialities, not really caring what or whether we ate. Blake ordered for us both a prawn cocktail entrée followed by cauliflower soup, then crown of lamb and vegetables for main course. We had just finished our main course when as if on cue, the band began to play "Turn Back the Hands of Time." Blake took my hand and led me onto the dance floor, his arms encircled me, "relax" he whispered as he held me very close and we danced as one our steps matching perfectly, unaware of anyone else, the magic of the moment was upon us. When the music stopped there was a huge ovation, little did we know all the other dancers had left the floor, sensing there was some special significance in our dance. The closeness of our dancing had fanned the flame, the longing and desire for each other was a burning flame coursing through our veins, demanding to be satisfied. We could feel the many pairs of curious eyes upon us as Blake guided me back to our table and instructed the waiter that we would have cheese and greens and coffee in our suite. Blake then led me from the dining room and to the lift as he pressed the start button, I imagined that hand fondling my breasts and exploring every inch of my body and a fresh shiver of expectation surged through me, I wanted him so much. The doors opened at our suite and Blake unlocked the door and kicked it shut behind us tearing his tie off as he strode to the adjoining bedroom. I rushed into my walk-in robe taking my clothes off and slipping into a filmy blue negligee. The powerful, aching want becoming almost unbearable in its need to be fulfilled. I waited and then came the gentle knock, the door opened and Blake, looking devastatingly handsome in a black silk robe which was undone and revealed his toned torso and manhood stood with arms outstretched. His arms encircled me as he bent his head and my lips parted involuntarily, his kiss opened the floodgates, the sun, the moon, and the stars were exploding around me as our robes slipped from us, I could feel his manhood rising with urgency, wave upon wave of burning want and emotion coursed through our entwined bodies. We stumbled to the bed, weak with desire, as the tumultuous need consumed us, my body was opening to his manhood like a flower in full bloom, waiting, waiting for pollination, then the exquisite joy as we gave and took of each other, harmony in our rhythmic pulsating consuming us as we climaxed in perfect unison. The love and longing of 42 years consummated in our joyous union. We just couldn't get enough of each other our bodies briefly calmed the desire for more of each other remained. We caressed and fondled each other, and the smoldering flame fanned by Blake's butterfly kisses over my body soon ignited, the rapture and delirium of urgent want was again coursing through our bodies only to be satisfied by the merging of our bodies in glorious love as we again throbbed in unison to ultimate culmination. We sealed our union with lingering kiss that long lost magic was there. Totally spent our bodies slowly relaxed, and we drifted off to sleep in each other's arms.

# Soul Mates Caressing

In the morning I awoke to Blake's gentle caressing kisses, the warm sun streaming in the window, was no match for the wave of hot emotion flooding me as Blake's kisses continued down my body pausing on one breast and then the other until totally titillated, I ached for his burgeoning manhood to again be within me. The smoldering flame of our night of passion now ignited as in dedication and joy we again merged our bodies in perfect harmony. Blake whispered against my lips "My darling adorable Laura, you are amazing, I knew you were my soul mate 42 years ago and nothing has changed". "Blake, darling, you have always been tucked away in my heart, the place I went to when life seemed unbearable, I have always known you were my soul mate, to have found each other again is so wonderful."

The coffee, cheese and greens that had been placed on the table by the fire, were still there, untouched next morning. The greens limp, the cheese cracked and dry from the warmth of the fire.

# A Day in the City

After a refreshing shower and dressing in casual clothes we sat out on the balcony and enjoyed the delicious fruit juice and croissants that Blake had ordered. The Advertiser was delivered with our breakfast. Blake was interested in reading it just as I was always eager to know what was going on in the world. Blake said he would like to get The Melbourne Herald, so he could keep up with news from there. I felt sure this could be arranged, we just needed to ask the desk clerk. We decided to spend the day in the city as Blake hadn't visited Adelaide for many years. We also needed to make some plans for the next few days, whether we stuck to them or not was irrelevant.

We headed down to Jetty Road to the tram terminal and hopped on the next tram going into the city. We got out at North Terrace. A delicious smell of coffee pervaded the air and we without speaking stepped into the café and Blake ordered two cappuccinos. Blake had not seen the bridge across the Torrens nor the revamped Adelaide oval, so we walked across and after viewing the Adelaide oval continued along the lawns behind the University toward the Zoo and Botanical Gardens. Blake was happy to indulge my love of animals. We strolled round the Zoo, hand in hand, watching the animals and their antics. The beautiful, elegant giraffes were stretching up to their food on the high poles. On to the elephants where the mother was nosing her new calf into the wallow, he got the message and rolled in the mud. We continued slowly on our way past animals and the birds, at last we were at the monkeys' cages where we were captivated by their antics. Then to the, oh so human like, chimpanzees, whom I could happily watch for hours. "Blake gently kissed me, as I looked up one of the chimps put his hand over his eyes, but peeped through his fingers, it was so cute. "Oh! Blake, look, we are embarrassing the chimp."

# Planning Time

We chatted and planned our week as we ambled along and over to the Botanic Gardens, they were so beautiful with the elegant tall trees, Morton Bay figs spreading their huge sheltering coppice above the many multi coloured flowerbeds beneath. There was a wedding happening, what a great place for a wedding I thought. The restaurant in the gardens was very busy with wedding guests it seemed. Maybe they were having their wedding reception there. My thoughts ran wild for a while. To marry Blake here would be a dream come true, the soft fresh lawn and the beautiful flowers on either side. I could see myself walking down to the man of my dreams, the man I loved and desired above all else. I visualized grandson Dale holding my hand as he walked me down to Blake. Dale was my eldest grandchild, and the others were too young for this honour. I continued my reverie what I would wear I wanted to look sexy and desirable yet modest. Blake brought me out of my reverie. The day was drawing to a close when he said "we better be getting back as I am taking you out for dinner tonight. Will you wear that blue dress?." I was surprised at this as I had another beautiful cocktail dress which I had bought and was itching to wear. The blue dress with its portrait neckline and form hugging skirt, with its split halfway up the left leg was quite sexy, maybe that is why he wanted me to wear it again. We headed up to North Terrace and caught the tram back to Glenelg.

# The Gift

After a refreshing shower I donned the blue dress, as he called it, again and walked out to the lounge where Blake was waiting for me. His blue eyes were smoldering with desire as he ran his eyes up and down my body. I wondered if we would even get to go out to dinner. "Looking at you excites me you are so beautiful and so desirable." "I have a gift for you, I designed it myself especially for you." He put the beautiful diamond necklace around my neck and fastened the catch. I looked in the mirror and the diamonds glittered. It was so beautiful, the diamonds linked into a heart shape with a beautiful pink diamond the main feature I turned to thank Blake as he reminded me that he had booked a taxi for 6.30. I hugged him tightly pressing his buttocks to me as I kissed his cheek. Hoping he realized this was a promise of more to come. There was no time to muse over the beauty of the necklace as the desk clerk had rung to say our cab was waiting.

I was curious but didn't ask where we were going. We went down to the foyer, there was a limousine out the front and that was our taxi. As we drove, I was soon able to work out that we were going to The Mount Osmond

Country Club. We were given the VIP treatment when we arrived and ushered to a candlelit table for two. Obviously, Blake had prearranged the menu as a fruit cocktail was soon in front of us, this was followed by a bowl; of mushroom soup, after sharing a bottle of champagne and eating our main course of seasoned Quail and vegetables Blake said, "Shall we go out and look over Adelaide lights now before dessert"? "Great idea" I replied. We were leaning on the balcony rail when Blake said, "You are amazing Laura, would you consider coming over to Melbourne"? I wasn't expecting that and after a pause I said I would think about it. Was this going to be a relationship with a week or two here, a week or two over in Melbourne and expensive gifts of jewelry? I knew I wanted more than that. I wanted a commitment and to know that he loved me. I loved and wanted him so much I craved his caresses and his body cuddling mine. I was disgusted with my thoughts and intense yearning for him. I needed to know we were compatible and that it was more than just a sexual relationship that he wanted.

Returning to the Dining room we opted not to have dessert but cheese and greens with a coffee, while we waited for our Limo. Both busy with our thoughts. Maybe it was too soon to expect a declaration or firm commitment.

On the drive down the winding hill Blake held me tight as we swayed to and from with the motion of the car, exciting my emotions which were rising to a crescendo of desire. Back in our suite and in bed, our hunger for each other took over and we made glorious love the intensity and pleasure consuming us. The subject of me going to Melbourne forgotten.

# Casual Day

Next day as planned, we headed off to McLaren Vale and did a tour of the district and its wineries. The concierge had our car ready for us and we were soon on our way. We had lunch at the Serafino Winery, before going on to Angove winery for more tasting. On to Bekkers Cellar Door Sales where we enjoyed a cheese platter, served with the wines. Then a strong black coffee before driving back to Glenelg. There was time for a short walk along the beach before for dinner. We paddled along towards West Beach and decided we would have a casual dinner at the beach front restaurant there. It was lovely to look out to sea with the sun setting as the tide rolled in. An ocean liner was sailing east and soon would disappear over the horizon. Were the passengers on the trip of a lifetime or young people seeking fun and hoping for a shipboard romance? A cargo ship was making its way toward Outer Harbour its size and various coloured containers now growing visible. The fading sun was glistening on the white capped waves as the tide continued to roll in booming as it reached the breakwater.

We enjoyed whiting and a tasty salad with a bottle of Reisling and the friendly atmosphere of the café. We bought a double ice-cream, one side strawberry the other chocolate, to eat on the short walk back along the esplanade. The stars twinkling and moon reflecting in the water were beautiful and created a romantic air, not that we needed it such was the burning feeling passing through our linked hands, we needed to curb our urge and calm our bodies. We planned an early night as next day we were travelling to Victor Harbor, which was one of my teenage holiday haunts. The early night happened but once in bed our passion and desire for each other took over.

After an early breakfast of croissants and fresh fruit and a quick look at the Advertiser we asked the concierge to have my car ready for us to head off. I felt quite nostalgic, as we drove down the hill into Victor, remembering how we used to play tennis and then go surfing at Port Elliott.

Blake motored down past the tennis courts and lawns, the beautiful Norfolk Pines casting their shade upon the families having lunch there. Blake turned into the Main Street past the Avoca Del where I had enjoyed many delicious ice-cream sodas as a teenager. Then on past The Victor Hotel to the car park by the causeway and luckily got a park there.

We walked out along the causeway to Granite Island. The surf thundering in onto the rocks and the spray rising far into the air was a spectacular sight. We continued on round the island, the cold wind was exhilarating, the fairy penguins peeped out from around their rocks I hadn't been to Granite Island since I was a teenager, and it brought back many happy memories of holidays shared with friends at Victor Harbour, and staying at the Clifton Guest House. Going to the pictures on a Wednesday and dances Friday and Saturday nights.

We were both feeling exhausted, some of the paths round the island were quite steep. We travelled on the horse tram across the causeway, the dear old Clydesdale pulled us safely back to shore. The café at the end of the causeway was busy, we waited our turn and bought a choc ice to sustain us for drive back to Glenelg. The exercise, sea air and the walk around the island had made us tired. I could easily have fallen asleep, that would not be fair I must to talk to Blake as he had to stay alert to drive. We needed to remember we were both over 60 and fit as we were, maybe we should have a quieter day tomorrow. Our active busy days and intense love making at night contributed to our tiredness.

We decided to have Dinner sent up to our suite and dine out on our balcony. The fresh fruit cocktail was refreshing, and we enjoyed the ham and salads main course. The moonlight reflecting on the water was as always romantic. The bottle of champagne we shared soon had its effect and we were feeling very relaxed as we reminisced over the day we had enjoyed together. So sleepy we went to bed, as always once in bed with our bodies so close and available to each other our desire took over, our tiredness was forgotten, and we made passionate love.

# Exploring

Our plans for the next day were to tour the Port area and visit the Maritime Museum. This was a very interesting place steeped in history. A boat trip on the Port River and seeing some dolphins at play added to the pleasure of the day. That evening we decided to do the roof top climb at the Adelaide Oval. This was an amazing experience and so scenic with the majestic St Peters Cathedral lit up for the night its' spires reaching to the sky, one side and the lights of the city twinkling the other. The tall buildings silhouetted against the night sky. Cars, looking like ants, traversing the roads through the city. We paused for a rest at the peak of the climb. Blake seemed preoccupied I asked, "what is on your mind Blake"? "I was wondering if you have had time to consider a trip over to Melbourne, I would really like to show you the sites of Melbourne and show you all it has to offer. Take you to some of the top restaurants and wine and dine you." "I am still thinking about it." Even though I really wanted to be with him, I needed to know our relationship was not just physical, I also knew I wanted something more permanent. We had enjoyed several excursions together and I did feel we were compatible and shared many of the same interests and ideals

After our busy day we showered and went straight to bed and talked about our amazing day together, so tired we drifted off to sleep our body's touching, and hands linked.

# Loving

I awoke in the morning to the warm sun streaming in the window, it was no match for the heat generated by Blake's loving gaze, I just melted into his arms, and we fulfilled our craven desire for each other; not wanting to draw apart we fondled each other. Blakes kisses lingering on my breasts, he was gently caressing my nipples' his tongue so soft, my whole body was arching toward his burgeoning manhood, which was soon within me, again we fulfilled our insatiable desire. I wondered if this was normal for people just over 60. I certainly wouldn't be asking any of my friends anything so personal. We enjoyed each other and our lovemaking so much who cares about anything else or what anyone else does in bed.

After sharing a shower and breakfast on the balcony we were off to the beach for the day. The weather was ideal, no wind, not too hot just a lovely spring day. We had fish and chips on the beach for our lunch the seagulls were hovering, and they had our leftovers. Squawking and flapping as they fought over the chips. A wind had sprung up and it was getting quite cool, so we went back to the suite and after a quick shower ate our dinner in the lounge by the log fire. We had such a lovely relaxing day and now I was fantasizing about the night ahead, God was I oversexed or just obsessed, feeling an urgent desire for his manhood. That fantasy was soon realized as we explored each other's body again and with rapturous delight mated.

# Crows v Geelong

"Would you like to go to the football tomorrow afternoon," Blake asked me next morning as he was reading the paper, "the Crows are playing Geelong." "wow! that would be great." I wondered what Blake would think of my barracking. As I got quite vocal and sometimes booed the umpires. Blake soon discovered I was an AFL addict and was happy to watch other games on the TV, which we had only turned on to watch the news and a couple of quiz shows.

We went to the Adelaide oval by tram and walked across the bridge with all the other fans streaming in. I was glad Blake had reserved our seats. The oval looked magnificent, so green and well mowed; the white lines stood out so white on the green grass. Their club banners were erected. Soon the players ran out through the banners stretching, jumping, and warming up, the siren sounded, and the captains moved to the centre for the toss. Another siren the first bounce and the game began. It was an exciting game with two very good teams battling for supremacy There was friendly rivalry between us as we barracked for our respective teams and this continued throughout the game, much

to my chagrin Geelong won. I felt tired and would quite
happily not gone out for dinner. Barracking, and the
excitement and tension had exhausted me. Blake had
planned a surprise dinner and he said I needed to dress
up and he hoped I would wear the diamond necklace. I
didn't want to spoil his plans and I hoped a shower would
refresh and revive me. I was happy to wear the necklace,
it was so beautiful and looked magnificent with the royal
blue lace dress with its wide neckline which I decided to
wear. A limo was waiting out the front when we went
down to the foyer. I had no idea where we were going,
Blake poured a Champagne each as we headed off. We
ended up at the Pavilion on the Park, having drunk a
bottle of champagne between us on the way I felt spaced
out. The waiter was ready for to take our order when we
arrived. I left the ordering to Blake, the champagne on an
empty stomach had me quite lightheaded. My head was
clearing, and I was enjoying the delicious roast Pork and
trimmings. The band playing a dreamy Modern Waltz
was quite romantic, Blake took my hand and led me
onto the floor his arms held me close, and we danced
as one; he whispered sweet endearments in my ear of
how much he enjoyed holding and the want it aroused
in him for more of me. Drawing apart we calmed our
desires and returned to our table and ordered dessert;
the fresh fruit salad topped with honey ice cream and
a meringue on top was delicious. A black coffee served
with a chocolate biscuit ended our meal. "I wonder if
Popeye still chugs up and down the river," I mused as
we waited, for the Limo, remembering the time so many

years ago when I had been taken for a ride with my sister and parents, and now you could even cook a BBQ whilst on the water. The Limo arrived and soon we were on our way back. I was thinking how Blake made me feel and the excitement I felt dancing with him, my desire for him was mounting. Could we make love in the Limo, the partition isolated the back seat from the front and the driver. I was disgusted with this thought was I becoming obsessed thinking only of the delight and pleasure sex was with Blake. Back at the Stamford Grande and up to our suite We were soon enjoying the demands made by our naked bodies.

The grandfather clock and town clock booming out 12 wafted in with the gentle sea breeze, through the open double doors of the balcony and totally sated we fell asleep.

# Showering

I wasn't really surprised when Blake suggested we go into the city again next day and see if Popeye did do the river trips, it did, and of course we did it. It was peaceful and scenic, the banks green and bright flowering shrubs either side on the riverbanks. We walked back and stopped at a café and bought a pie and freshly squeezed orange drink for our lunch, which we enjoyed as we sat on the grassy slope beside the river Torrens. A leisurely walk along North Terrace and past the magnificent War Memorial to King William Street, where we caught the tram back to Glenelg. I felt I needed a refreshing shower after our day out in the wind and the sun as did Blake.

Each bedroom had its own amenities however we decided to shower together and wash each other's backs. This soon extended to me washing Blake's rippling torso, which I especially enjoyed. He turned me to him and gently washed my breasts until I was totally titillated Showering together was so exciting and we succumbed to the urge for more of each other, making love in the shower added yet another delightful experience. The second bedroom and its ensuite was soon redundant. We usually showered together now and washed and dried each other, we both enjoyed this intimacy and the feelings it aroused for each other.

I felt quite tired, and I guess Blake did too as he suggested we have dinner sent up to us at 7:00pm to eat out on our balcony. No need to dress for dinner, so I donned my white silk negligee, it was so pretty with pink roses splashed over it and lace trim. Blake had changed into a black satin robe. He really was strikingly handsome, just to look at him made my heart beats quicken. Blake had ordered a bottle of Riesling which came with our dinner, he poured a glass each, mine tingled all the way down. The pumpkin soup with croutons was delicious as was the whiting and salad which followed. As Blake topped up our wine he said, "Laura, you amaze me more and more with your ability to enjoy and adapt to whatever we do. I love you, have you decided to come home to Melbourne with me?" "Yes. I will come. I'd like to see what Melbourne has to offer, it's a long time since I was last there, and of course I want to meet your family."

# Blake's Pad

As I had decided to go to Melbourne with Blake to meet his family and friends. I organized being away from the farm for another two weeks. Grandson Dale, was happy to continue to live at the farm and look after my animal menagerie and as he worked for his father this was not a problem.

Blake had now been away from his business for five weeks and needed to consult with Edward to ensure there were no problems. We flew back to Melbourne in Blake's private jet; the crew treated me like royalty I was not used to such luxury. Edward met us on our arrival at the airport and drove us to Blakes apartment, in Blake's car a Mercedes Benz. I was looking around as we drove, it was very busy cars seemed to be travelling in all directions at breakneck speed and the screech of brakes at times made me think there would be a crash. Edward drove into the private underground parking area which belonged to the Jackson Foundation, it also provided parking for his employees. Edward helped carry our bags to the lift and came up with us to Blake's apartment to have a coffee before going back to his office. It was a large and luxurious bachelor pad.

The kitchenette, which was equipped with all the modern appliances to make life easy, opened into the lounge area. A 65cm colour TV was affixed to one wall and two armchairs were conveniently placed side by side for viewing. A side table was by each chair. A door off the lounge led into a passage with a bedroom either side. one had a three-quarter bed in it and was obviously Blake's room. In the other was a King size bed which Blake had ordered for what would now be our room and which was still to be assembled and the new linen washed before the bed could be made and ready to sleep in. Blake thought we could sleep in his three-quarter bed for a few nights. I agreed, anticipating the closeness and joy of Blake wrapping his body around mine and holding me close. I loved and wanted him so much I craved his caresses and his body cuddling mine. Desire for him stirring in me at this thought. I was often disgusted with my intense desire for him.

An ensuite bathroom and a spacious walk-in robe adjoined the main bedroom. The pad was carpeted throughout with a cream and brown figured Axminster.

The coffee we had with Edward before he left for his office had refreshed us. We unpacked our bags before thinking about where we would have Dinner. Blake chose a little café close-by, and we walked the short distance. The staff knew Blake as he often had lunch there, and welcomed us warmly. We enjoyed a simple meal of tomato soup and garlic bread, not really very hungry we had a coffee and walked back to Blake's pad.

We shared a shower and towelled each other dry before getting into bed, I loved being nestled in his arms our closeness arousing our desire as we explored every inch of each other's body and I loved running my hands over his muscles and toned body, as he caressed me; the explosion of urgent want for him and his manhood demanding fulfilment.

# Family & Friends

Staying here provided ample opportunity to meet his family and friends. Blake wanted to show me several sights and to show me the beauty of the city. He wined and dined me at several restaurants. Cumulus Inc, Coda, Vue de Monde, a different one every night. This was so different to my home cooked dinners on the farm.

Blake's children and grandchildren were a delight and each of the family's invited us out for a day and a meal, I felt quite comfortable as they were very welcoming to me. They seemed glad their father had found happiness after five years of loneliness. I don't know if Blake told them of our teenage romance, and what happened to separate us and how he had found me again.

I coped well with Blake's friends, most of whom had their own businesses. I found listening was the best way to learn of their interests and understand them. They were keen to hear about my background and farm, and how I knew Blake. I told them we were old friends from our teenage years. I could see they were curious, but I wasn't forthcoming with any more information, it really wasn't their business.

Blake organized a Buffet Dinner at his Corporation for the following Friday night so he could introduce me to his employees. They were a happy group so obviously content in their employment and admiration and respect for Blake, and it was a very pleasant evening.

Edward text me next morning to say the employees all liked me and hoped I'd pop in again. That was good to hear.

# Marvel Stadium

The Crows would be playing Collingwood at Marvel stadium, on the next Saturday and Blake said he would take me if I would like to go. I certainly did, I was excited to be going to this amazing stadium, it was so much bigger than Adelaide. We arrived early and found our seats. I soon worked out why Blake wanted to be there early. It seemed like millions of people were coming in, the attendance was shown later at over 96000 people. Adelaide has a beautiful oval and surrounds but not the capacity of this stadium, 53000 was about the maximum at Adelaide oval. I thought again how thoughtful and kind Blake is, to get the tickets and take me as he isn't addicted to football like I am.

The game was exciting, the lead changing often throughout the game. It was so disappointing for me as the Crows lost by 2 points, which should not have happened as our key player was knocked down and bleeding from the nose, 70 seconds from full time, he should have got a free but didn't. I've always thought the umpires favour the Melbourne teams, especially Collingwood.

Blake also showed me many other sites including the Westgate Bridge and Little Collins Street and where

Tattersalls was, places I had visited when I was 18 and went to Melbourne with a girlfriend to see a comedy show at the Tivoli Theatre.

# The Proposal

Although we had dined at a different restaurant every night, all of them very elegant and with great cuisine. Blake said there was another restaurant he wanted to take me to, which was just out of the main city on the banks of the Yarra. It had a lovely outlook and was really a romantic setting. Our table was in a quiet candlelit corner, organized by Blake who had also preordered the meal. He knew I found some of the fancy names of the different courses confusing, I hadn't been wined and dined for so many years. The wine waiter was hovering, and Blake ordered champagne which was served with the usual flourish and as we sipped the tingling sensation was matching my feeling of anticipation. I don't know why I felt so excited.

The prawn entrée was very tangy, this was followed by a delicious minestrone soup with garlic bread. The band was softly playing a romantic Modern waltz, Blake took my hand and led me onto the dance floor, it was very crowded, so we decided to go out on the balcony for a while, the sea breeze was quite cool, and we soon went inside to our table. As soon as we sat down the waiter asked if we were ready for our main course, we nodded our assent. The seasoned duckling with apricot sauce, was delicious usually I wouldn't choose to eat duckling. I would have to compliment the chef. Dessert was Bomb Alaska; when the rum was poured over and lit the blue flames danced merrily in the candlelight. We had drunk two bottles of champagne, and a strong black coffee was a must before we left to go back to Blake's apartment. I soon realized we were on a different route, obviously Blake wanted to show me something else. We seemed to be ascending and were now looking over Melbourne. Blake seemed to be pre-occupied as he parked the car in a secluded spot well away from other sightseers. It was very romantic with the myriad of twinkling lights as they danced into the night sky from the tall buildings silhouetted against the sky.

He gathered me in his arms and hugged me so tight I could barely breathe then said "Laura, I love you with all my heart and soul will you marry me"? I gasped for breath and was able to say, "I adore you Blake and have always loved you, you've been tucked away in a corner of my heart, the place I went to when life was unbearable, I do want to marry you, but I don't want to live in the city." I knew I needed to tell Blake this. "Darling Laura you won't have to live in the city I have a Station which I bought as an investment when I was 25 years old and received my inheritance, always with the idea that I would retire there., "Blakes Haven" borders the banks of the river Murray not far from Renmark. I have had Managers at Blakes Haven over the years, and only went up occasionally to discuss business matters with the Manager from time to time. I was deliriously happy; the magic of Blake's proposal and the glorious setting would stay with me forever.

I modernized and redecorated the Gate House where I would stay on my short visits to see the Managers. I have a trusted friend and former employee Gordon, who with his wife Becky are now living there in the gate cottage as caretakers. Gordon, was a clever designer and maker of some of the finest jewelry of the Jackson Corporation. He suffered a hand injury which made it impossible to continue with his work. He and his wife Becky were happy to go into retirement as caretakers at Blake's Haven. They also looked after Blake's Labrador Baxter who couldn't live in the apartment when Blake moved from his house in the eastern suburbs after Grace died.

Blake wanted me to see "Blakes' Haven." He had always planned to restore it to its' former glory and to add a modern wing for his own use. I was feeling much happier, to marry Blake would be my dream come true and I knew I would be happy living out of the city. We drove to the station and at my first glimpse of the homestead I could see how magnificent it had been and would be again when restored.

We walked down to the river, it was so tranquil as the Murray flowed quietly by, the birds were singing and twittering in the trees. I felt like I had come home. I felt sure there would be plenty of space for Bonnie and Clyde my pet sheep, Bella my golden Labrador and Freddie my cat to come and live at "Blakes Haven." When Blake told me about "Baxter" I hoped another of my secret dreams might be realized. Maybe Baxter and Bella would become mates and reproduce, wouldn't that be great? Blake was amused but quite happy to let me follow this whim at a later date

The paddock which surrounded the orchard would be suitable for Bonnie and Clyde and they could eat the grass and the fruit that fell from the trees. My brain was in overdrive with ideas. Blake wanted to develop a wetland area with suitable grasses to encourage more waterbirds back to the area. A small section of the riverbank could be reclaimed and fenced off, it would be ideal. It seemed there was so much to think about and plan.

"I have to meet with my architect to consolidate plans for the renovations and additions which we will need to have done to the homestead. I want you to be a part of the planning." "I would love to be involved." It would be a huge task for the architect.

After a quick "Hallo and good-bye" to Gordon and Becky we left to drive back to Melbourne. We chatted about the homestead and were keen to see what the architect would formulate. "I also bought a small airplane aircraft which is housed at an airfield near Sydney. They maintain it, at my expense, it is used for short sightseeing flights, the income going to the Royal Flying Doctor Service. I take it for a flight occasionally to keep my Pilots License current. We could fly back to Angaston whenever you wanted to for a visit." This was an unexpected surprise.

# Wedding Plans

Having all the plans in place for the restoration of "Blakes Haven" it was time to go back to Adelaide and to break the news of our impending marriage to my children and their families.

After saying Goodbye to Blake's family, we flew back to Adelaide. We would have a week in Adelaide to enjoy some quiet time together and make some arrangements. The staff at the Stamford Grande were beginning to know us and greeted us warmly.

In the morning we agreed not much planning would be done if we stayed in our suite. After breakfast of fruit, croissants, and coffee we showered and went walking. That way we could plan as we walked. To some this might seem premature but having known each other so well 42 years ago and knowing all we wanted was each other and to be together was enough for us.

We caught the tram into the city and revisited the Botanic Gardens, as of one accord we decided this would be the spot for our wedding. "Can we be ready in 3 weeks" Blake asked. We needed to seek permission, organize a celebrant, and get a marriage license. "If we can get all the preparations in place, why not" I said. As Blake had booked the suite for another three weeks, with an optional fourth we were able to make the arrangements and organize our marriage. I said, "Blake are we rushing things"? "I, am sure we are not; we have loved each other for over 42 years why waste any more time"?

# Meeting My Family

Next week Blake came with me to my farm at Angaston and met my family. My children and their families popped in several times during the week and Blake soon endeared himself to them. Nicholas and Thomas took him around the vineyard and the farms, he was interested in all aspects of the growing of the grapes and the wine making. The sheep stud was also very interesting for him as he hadn't realized how much documentation was needed in recording sires and ewes and the progeny. Blake had vivid memories of living with his family at Mt Pleasant and the sheep stud they had, he was too young, at 9 when his family were all killed, to remember much about the recording involved in a stud but had always hoped to establish one at "Blakes Haven" when he retired.

Kate and Helen also invited us for a meal and Blake met all the grandchildren as they included the boys and their families. The week passed in a whirl of excitement and some necessary planning. Dale was happy to make my farm his home and look after everything.

I invited two close friends and their husbands to dinner the following Saturday. We had a great night, and it was as if they had known Blake for years. He just fitted in so well. I had known these friends since schooldays and confided in them years ago that George and my marriage existed in name only. They certainly knew George spent most of his time at the 19h hole at the Golf club, and had guessed that our marriage existed in name only long before I told them. They knew that I spent a lot of time in the garden and keeping myself fit with sport and gym. I had told them Blake and I had known each other over 42 years ago.

We returned to Adelaide, then it was back to Melbourne for more planning for our honeymoon, also another meeting with the architect.

# Honeymoon Plans

We had decided on a world cruise for our honeymoon, and this needed to be booked. We went to the Flight Centre and booked on the first available world Cruise which was on the Princess Royal and leaving 2 days after our wedding.

I was worried about my clothes as I lived in jeans and shirts on the farm and tailored slacks and shirts for outings in my country lifestyle. There was not a lot of need for day dresses or after five frocks. Blake gave me his credit card and said, "go and buy whatever you fancy, money is no object." I didn't really need Blake's credit card as I was quite wealthy in my own right but if it made him happy then I would do as he suggested. Camille took me under her wing and introduced me to the right Boutiques and stores and soon had me glammed up for the cruise. Camille enjoyed the excitement of the shopping spree just as much as I did. I knew most of my excitement was related to our coming honeymoon and the time Blake and I would spend together in our suite.

# The Homestead

The homestead needed a complete facelift. The dining room was plenty big enough for the Corporate Dinners, which Blake would host from time to time, for his business associates and their wives, but sadly in need of repair. A huge cedar table with 14 accompanying chairs all needed restoration, the tapestry seats of the chairs needed replacing. A small lounge off the dining room would be ideal for coffee and business discussions. The large kitchen adjoining the dining room, needed a complete overhaul and new stoves, fridges, freezers, everything that would accommodate the whims of any chef who was employed to cater for these Corporate Dinners. A toilet and bathroom with access from the main Dining room and a lounge needed to be in the plan. The veranda and steps leading into the house were all slate and in need of repair. It would be a very imposing entrance to the foyer when restored.

The old guest wing had four large bedrooms all needed redecorating and ideally ensuites installed. New carpets throughout this wing. Our wing would be modernized. The bedroom with an ensuite plus walk-in robe. The large bay window would stay and two chairs, a table and small bar fridge added. An open space living area with lounge and dining table, with a small compact kitchen. A Den/library for Blake, big enough to house his desk, books and wine rack, and a Studio for me, where I could write, or paint whichever mood was upon me these would need to be built on. An open fireplace in our living area where we could relax and Baxter, Bella and Freddie could be with us in winter.

A patio with BBQ area and access to a swimming pool, with changing facilities, and an exercise and games room, backed by a garden shed and toilet with access from games room and garden.

We wanted it to be environmentally friendly as much as possible, availing use of natural light and warmth. Skylights would be installed wherever possible. Kennels for the Bella and Baxter, an area for Bonnie and Clyde to roam and a few hens. The orchard which was well established and fenced would be fine for them. Sweeping lawns, a fountain, a rose garden in front of the house and surrounding the fountain and lawned area native shrubs, provision for a vegetable garden with raised garden beds at the back. Blake and I were both keen to grow our own vegetables and herbs. It seemed never ending. It was going to be quite a task for the Architect, he would certainly earn his money.

# The Architect

In Melbourne for a few more days, to meet the architect and slowly we mapped out a more specific idea of what we wanted. He would work on it and hopefully through emails be able to finalize the plan and get the work started before we got back from our cruise.

We engaged an interior decorator to take care of the furnishing etc., giving her an outline for colour schemes and general décor. I suggested that we go with regency striped curtains in the magnificent dining room which had a beautiful ceiling and cornices in keeping with the age of the homestead. The huge mahogany dining table and chairs, which had belonged to the station owners had been left there, and were to be restored to their former glory, all of this we asked the interior decorator to organize.

It was now only a week until our wedding and I needed to go home to Angaston to finalize a few business matters. We just did not want to be apart but had to be.

# Wedding Outfit

I had decided that Kate and Helen should help me pick out my wedding outfit. They met me at the airport, and we hit the shops. I was delighted with my indigo blue shantung outfit and quirky little fascinator. The short lace jacket looked great over the very slim fitting dress, the side split in the skirt was sexy, yet modest. My earlier reverie would now happen as Dale would take my hand and walk with me down the path to where my lover, the man of my dreams waited. The excitement and anticipation for what lay ahead was mounting.

My boys were already set up and happy, Thomas with his vineyard and Nicholas with his farm. Dale was more than happy to continue living in my home as he wanted to be independent of his parents. I had taught him the specifics of recording the stud sheep and their progeny, he felt confident to take on this responsibility. It did not take long to sort my business affairs out.

I could change all my banking details and other business matters when we returned from our honeymoon cruise. We would be cruising for 3 months.

# At Last

Our wedding day arrived. We were again booked into The Stamford Grand Hotel, where we dressed and where Nicholas met me with Dale who would walk with me down the path to the man of my dreams, the man I had always loved, the man I loved beyond all else. Our families were assembled, and the celebrant was there waiting for us. Dale held my hand as we walked along the lush green lawn between the multi coloured flower beds to the tune of Eternal Love. Blake turned to greet me his hand outstretched to take my hand. I was so happy to be marrying this handsome, thoughtful, and considerate man who shared so many of my ideals and interests.

We had each written our vows to each other and as we stood before the Celebrant an overwhelming sense of peace and happiness descended upon me. After the preliminaries, the celebrant asked me to present my vows. "Blake you are my soul mate, you have always had a place in my heart, I adore you, I promise to love, cherish and care for you for the rest of my life." It was now Blake's turn. "Laura darling, my soul mate, I promise to love you, honour you, cherish and care for you and will worship you all the days of my life." With those simple vows we were pronounced man and wife. We exchanged rings, made of course by the Jackson Corporation. Mine to match the beautiful diamond ring Blake had given me when I agreed to marry him and which he himself had designed and crafted.

We were given many good luck tokens by the younger grandchildren and after hugs and kisses all round we headed back to the Stamford Grand for our wedding luncheon. This was a very happy and somewhat noisy occasion as the younger grandchildren entertained us with an impromptu concert. Our goodbyes were said, and the families headed off, mine in their cars and Blake's to the airport where Blake's private jet waited to fly them back to Melbourne. The jet was really for business purposes and the long overseas journeys made by the Marketing Director and Director of Purchases, and only used occasionally for special private events. Tired but oh so happy, we went up to our suite.

The bed was covered with red rose petals and a bottle of champagne awaited us. We toasted each other and gently kissed, undressed, and lay on the bed our bodies touching, igniting our desire, our tiredness soon forgotten submitting to the excruciating ache of want as our bodies were inflamed by the surging current of need for each other. Blake's kisses further inflamed my desire, I ached for him, his manhood was soon within me filling me with rapture and delight as in perfect sync we celebrated our official union.

We flew back to Melbourne next morning and to Blake's apartment, where we would spend the next two days before leaving on our cruise.

# Honeymooning

The two days quickly passed, with meetings with the Architect, consultations with builders and generally tidying things up before we departed. Blake spent time with Edward ensuring all was in order with the business. With laptops and emails problems could be solved if any occurred. A quick trip up to "Blake's Haven" to see Becky and Gordon, fill them in on coming events and make sure they were well and happy. They are such a lovely couple, so friendly and welcoming, just like old friends to me as they are to Blake. Their respect and genuine admiration for Blake was mirrored in their faces.

Edward picked us up and took us to the airport where we would fly to Sydney to board the Princess Royal. We walked up the gangway and on board, a lift took us up to our level and balcony executive suite, which gave us the privacy to sunbake or read if we chose and to be alone. It was wonderful to just relax after the whirlwind of the last few weeks. We decided to dine on our balcony the first night. After a fresh fruit entrée and main course of barramundi and salad washed down with champagne, we opted not to have dessert. The air was balmy and the moonlight dancing on the waves was a beautiful sight, the occasional white cap adding to the beauty. Blake was holding me close and nuzzling my neck, he romantically said I was the only dessert he wanted. The love of our teenage years which we had been denied, now rekindled raged through our bodies demanding to be satisfied.

We went into our cabin and Blake held me close enjoying our togetherness as slowly we undressed each other, we didn't need any foreplay however we indulged ourselves until we could no longer contain our urge for fulfilment.

# In the Raw

I enjoyed sleeping in the raw with Blake, it just seemed so right, our bodies touching, free and available to each other at all times. Just the touch of Blake's skin against me was enough, but we caressed and fondled each other, he always knew just where to put his hands until the want was unbearable, and we merged our bodies, celebrating our first night away from all sight and sound of others. The gentle rocking of the ship lulled us off to sleep and after the whirlwind of the last 8 weeks we slept soundly.

Next day after a leisurely breakfast on our balcony we decided to stroll around the ship and to see what activities were available. We enjoyed a game of deck tennis, then a game of quoits and met some other couples. We also enrolled at the Gym for two sessions each a week

That night we were invited to dine at the captain's table, we couldn't really refuse although that was not what we had planned. The dinner was of course perfect and with a few special toasts to each other, we were very relaxed and wanting to be alone. The band struck up a waltz to dance was expected. We'd just started dancing when the captain tapped Blake on the shoulder and so he had to surrender me to him, and Blake to dance with Captain's little dumpling of a wife. As soon as we could we excused ourselves and went back to our suite. Anticipation was surging through us as we closed the door and Blake's arms engulfed me, our bed was turned down ready for us and we wasted no time in getting in and the release of our desire was simultaneous and as always so unique in its consuming joy. It seemed our desire and hunger for each other was insatiable.

I felt embarrassed that our age we had such a craven desire for each other and at the insatiable intensity of our lovemaking as we gave and took of each other and the final glorious moment the explosion of joy as we climaxed in perfect unison. Blake said we had over 42 years to catch up so let's enjoy and live the moment. Next day we would go ashore at Brisbane.

# Brisbane Onward

We decided to do a river cruise which would take us under all the bridges and stop off at Elizabeth Street for a look. It was very hot, and both having been to Brisbane before on more than one occasion we decided to get back on the river boat and go back to the Princess Royal. It was great to be back in the airconditioned comfort of our suite and enjoy a glass of refreshing orange juice. Tired but happy we both dozed off. It was much later when we awoke, and Blake ordered a cold serve for our dinner which we ate out on our balcony. The sky was yellow with all the lights of Brisbane and the reflections in the water twinkling below us. Soon we would be leaving Brisbane.

Bali, Singapore, Phuket, Sri Lanka, across to the Suez Canal, Egypt, Naples, Rome, Italy, Athens - Greece, Anzac Cove, Spain, Portugal, Malta, The Greek Islands, and we also cruised the Danube. We had a quick tour of England, Seeing Buckingham Palace; Trafalgar Square, Big Ben and of course walking the bridge over the Thames. New York, Miami down through the Panama Canal to Lima across to Easter Island, Pitcairn Island, Tahiti then Auckland Just some of the amazing places we visited before we sailed back home to Sydney. So many exciting and interesting places to talk about and reminisce on in the future. When the ship berthed at the different ports there was usually a small bus or taxi touting for us to ride with them and visit the tourist attractions.

Whenever we were anchored in a harbour and had the opportunity to spend some time on shore, we did so, that way we could talk to the locals and find out first-hand about their country and their customs.

I will never forget Lombok, their farming on the terraced hillsides fascinated both of us. We sampled their food as we walked the village. The beautiful modern hotels were a surprise obviously for the tourists. The humid climate took its toll, and we were very tired by the end of the excursion and glad to get back to our airconditioned suite.

# On Board

There were plenty of coffee parlours, and wine bars conveniently placed around the ship. Every night there was entertainment in each of the theatres on board. Musicals, song and dance, comedy shows we usually attended one of them. The Atrium, which had a grand piano, was also a popular spot, the pianist would play requests and the drink waiter took orders and delivered. Sometimes we went there with other couples. We had spent more time with one couple, Claudia, and Jordan Davey, with whom we had more in common. They had recently sold up their large property in the wheat belt of Western Australia near Esperance and were planning to retire at Cottesloe after a trip around Australia. They were going to buy a motor home after the cruise and planned to be on the road for at least a year. It sounded like a good idea.

Christmas on board was quite amazing the stewards decorated and whole ship with fairy lights and Christmas wreaths and streamers festooned the walkways and stairs. A huge Christmas tree, glowing with tinsel and coloured lights took pride of place in the Atrium.

After Christmas Dinner, which we shared with others at the captain's table, we all moved down to the Atrium.

Father Christmas arrived and sat in front of the tree, he had a huge sack and handed out lollies and Christmas crackers to those who went and sat on his knee.

New Years's eve was also an amazing night the Christmas decorations remained, and mistletoe was hung in many places. The young couples on board made good use of the opportunity to kiss and cuddle.

There was a big clean up after these celebrations and shipboard life returned to normal. We realized we only had three weeks left before we would be sailing into Sydney Harbor and then flying home.

We made the most of being waited on and enjoying the meals provided either in the cafeteria or the main dining room. We also spent more time with shipboard acquaintances especially Claudia and Jordan Davey. We hoped to catch up with each other sometime in the future and exchanged phone numbers.

# Home Again

We flew back to Melbourne and Edward met us and took us back to the apartment. Blake went into the business next day, while I shopped for some necessary provisions before we went to Blakes Haven.

Blake had kept in touch via email with the architect while we were away and Blakes Haven was almost finished the builders only had a few small adjustments to make. "Felicity" our interior decorator was keen to arrange for the painting, floor covers, furniture, and drapes etc. to be brought in. She was to supervise this, so we didn't have to worry, just keep checking that we were happy. We wanted to be at Blakes Haven and once again we were availing ourselves of Gordon and Becky's hospitality as we kept an eye on the progress. At last Felicity said we should bring our personal pieces and pictures in. I flew back to Adelaide where Nicholas met me and took me up to Angaston. It was lovely to see them all and catch up with all the grandchildren. That done, Thomas loaded his trailer with the furniture and personal treasures *I wanted,* and Nicholas loaded Bonnie and Clyde and an outdoor setting, Bella would travel with Thomas and his family and Freddie, and I would go with Nicholas and his family. We headed off early for our journey to "Blakes Haven" and Blake was there to meet us. Once the trailers were un-loaded, we enjoyed a lovely BBQ with salads prepared by Becky and relaxed around the swimming pool. It developed into a housewarming party as Kate, Helen and their families arrived, and Blake's family came up from Melbourne. It was great to see both of our families getting on so well. Next morning after a hearty brunch the families left to travel to their respective homes. I was keen to sort out my treasures which the boys had brought over and find the right spot to put them. Blake helped me after checking on Baxter and Bella; they seemed to be getting on well together. Bonnie and Clyde were happy in their paddock which had a variety of mature fruit trees and reached right down to the river. Freddie had made himself quite at home on his cushion in my study.

We felt like getting outside in the fresh air. Hand in hand we strolled down to the river, it was so peaceful watching the Murray flow gently by, the birds twittering and chirping in the gum trees added to the ambience. The day was warming up, so we strolled back to the house for a drink and relax in the living room, exhausted with the excitement and activity of the last few days we both nodded off. It was dusk when we awoke and decided to invite Gordon and Becky up for supper. They were happy to come, and we had an enjoyable evening together. Blake told them we wanted to be known as Kaine's, Blake's family name, and that Jackson was the business name only.

On our second night in our new home the desire and urgency of our magnetism and want were there impatiently wanting to be satisfied. There was champagne in the fridge in the Bay window of our bedroom where two chairs and a little table were set up. We toasted each other before going to bed and as usual the joy and harmony of our mating was beautiful in our forever home.

Our sex life was always spontaneous, a touch, a look, a word was all we needed for a burning want to surge through our bodies demanding more.

# Getting a Gardener

We were eager to explore the kitchen garden, which was almost non-existent, we realized we needed a trip into Renmark to purchase some seeds and plants. We wanted to do this ourselves. We both enjoyed gardening and to grow and pick our own herbs and fresh vegetables was our plan.

A gardener and landscaper had been engaged to do the front garden, we needed to tell him we were home and ready to meet with him to discuss the plans so he could begin.

We went to the Newsagents to see if we could get the Advertiser and the Herald dropped off at our gate by the school bus which we had noticed went past our gate. Having ascertained this could happen we picked up some grocery supplies and headed home. Our mornings were falling into a pattern, a walk down to the gate to pick up the papers and then back to the den for a coffee and read the papers. I liked to do the crosswords and sudoku and discovered that Blake also was a keen crossword solver. He sometimes helped me when I was stuck on a word clue and sometimes, I helped him.

We had purchased a 65cm TV so that we could watch the AFL or the Cricket, and of course the news and a few Quiz shows. We both liked to pit our knowledge against the contestants on a Quiz show.

We arranged to have a mailbox and it wasn't long before the word got around and we were receiving invitations to different clubs and meetings. I decided "Book Club" and "The Hospital Auxiliary" would be enough for me at present and Blake decided on "Rotary" and "Men's Shed." We both enjoyed being home and strolling down to the river where Blake had his old tinny moored at our landing and I was happy to sit and read in my driftwood chair which Blake had made. The animals always followed. We now had some hens in the orchard, and they too would come down following Bonnie and Clyde, and Bella and Baxter.

We received an invitation from a neighbour for a social afternoon. This was an opportunity to meet with them and the other locals they had invited we really enjoyed ourselves. They were obviously curious but didn't pry. Soon we were receiving more invitations from neighbours and clubs. In truth we were more than happy just spending our time together after all the years we had missed, however the friendliness being shown to us could not be ignored, and of course would be reciprocated at a later date.

Blake had joined the "Men's Shed" which met once a month. Members helped with projects for less fortunate families and their children in the community. This he felt was worthwhile. He was particularly drawn to a lad called Tom whose father had died in a boating accident and the circumstances reminded Blake of his early years and the sadness and loneliness he had endured. Tom loved fishing and Blake was happy to take him out in his tinnie, occasionally Tom caught a cod, which Blake helped him clean, so he could take it home to his mother to cook for their tea.

Men's shed nights became my "Book Club" night several other wives came along, and we enjoyed discussions on books we had read and a light supper, we met a different person's home each month, when at your home you provided the supper and a coffee or champagne.

Our garden was taking shape now, so we decided to invite all the neighbours to a BBQ lunch by the pool. I knew they wanted to see inside but I wasn't ready yet as I still had some unpacking and sorting out to complete. It was a pleasant day, and they were all interesting and friendly people. Blake cooked marinated steak, chops and sausages and the marinated chicken kebabs which I had made. Plenty of onion added to the tasty meal, along with a tossed green salad and garlic bread.

# Claudia & Jordan

We spent a lot of time out in the garden, often sitting beneath the large shady gum trees we were doing just that when we saw a motor home driving in. I was such a pleasant surprise to see our shipboard friends Claudia and Jordan Davey. They stayed two days, and we enjoyed hearing about their travels, they were now homeward bound after a year on the road. It was so lovely to see them, and we put a visit to Western Australia on our to do list.

# Rotary Ball

The Rotary Ball was coming up and also the Hospital Ball. An urgent SOS to Camille for a couple of suitable gowns I would leave the selection to her. I was delighted with the royal blue delustered satin she had chosen, and the burnished gold embroidered taffeta and they fitted perfectly. Camille knew what would suit me and had made very good choices. The District Governor and his wife would be attending the Rotary Ball, and Presidents and their wives of neighboring Rotary Clubs would also be invited.

As we were dressing for the Rotary Ball, I thought how handsome and distinguished Blake looked in his Dinner suit. I felt great in the royal blue satin, one shoulder and arm were inset with organza and the other was adorned with a large satin bow. I hoped it wasn't too daring, I put on my diamond necklace and was very happy with my overall appearance. Blake said "you look amazing you take my breath away" we were both back in the past momentarily, but knew we must leave, it wouldn't do to be late as the District Governor was coming. I hadn't felt this excited about a Ball since I was a teenager, remembering all the beautiful ball gowns my mother made for me.

Pre-ball drinks were being hosted by the local President and his wife. We got a surprise when the District Governor and his wife arrived it was Colin, Blakes old friend from Savings Bank days. They had lost touch years ago. There was some surprise on Colin's face, and immediate recognition when he was introduced to me. I felt sure we would be seeing more of them at a later date. It is amazing how people crop in your life at the most unexpected time. Colin knew about our past and what had happened and would without a doubt be very curious as to how we were now married.

The ball was a huge success with pomp and ceremony, we were formally announced as we arrived "Rotarian Blake Kaine and his wife Laura." I thought how nice that sounded. We would have liked to dance together all night but as others asked me to dance Blake asked their wife and so the night went on until midnight and the last dance the medleys. It had been an exciting night and we both felt tired as we drove home. During the evening Colin and his wife invited Blake and I to come to lunch the following Sunday, they lived near Renmark so it wasn't far to travel, we expected that Colin would be curious as to how we eventually married as he knew we were in love and that my father had sent Blake packing and out of my life all those years ago.

# Reminiscing

Colin and Blake did plenty reminiscing about old times and the bank teller days, while I chatted with his wife Beth. Beth was a keen gardener, and she took me around their extensive grounds, they employed a gardener who came for 3 hours a week. I asked his name as I knew we would need to get one as ours was now too big for Blake and me to manage. Colin was obviously curious as to how Blake and I were now married. Without going into too much detail Blake said after his wife died and George died, fate took a hand. I think he would have liked to know how but did not pry. We might open up about it at a later date. It would sound bizarre to some. Colin and Blake talked about Rotary and the fortnightly meeting coming up at which Colin would be seeking Rotary families to host an exchange student from America. It was an enjoyable day, and we arranged to occasionally meet them for lunch on our shopping days and of course we would invite them to Blakes Haven.

As we travelled home Blake mentioned hosting an exchange student and asked how I felt about it. I would be very happy as I remembered when my father was a Rotarian and we hosted and American girl and what a delight she was. At the next meeting Blake told them we would be happy to host if needed. Tired but happy, we shared a champagne and slept soundly.

# Family Visits

We had a phone call from Nick. He had arranged for Thomas and Kate and Helen and all the grandchildren to come for a weekend visit. We were delighted and a date was arranged. We were able to get a chef for the weekend and we gave him license to organize the menu and supplies needed. Our first opportunity to use the magnificent dining room. The children were keen to try water skiing on the river and Blake arranged this, he had bought a motorboat which would be ideal. All we needed to do was get some water skis, which Blake said he would get before their next visit. Meantime they could skim along on tires pulled by ropes attached to the motorboat.

It was a wonderful weekend, and the dining room had its first "dinner" I was so glad as Blake said he wouldn't need to have corporate dinners as Edward would host them in Melbourne. Family celebrations would be enjoyed in the spacious room. We planned to invite some of the neighbours, to dinner to repay their hospitality and this would be another opportunity to use the dining room.

We knew Edward, Camille, Kirsty, and their families were coming up soon, which will be great, and another chance to use the beautiful dining room.

Blake had bought two sets of water skis and decided he would build a boat shed where his motorboat, the skis a fridge and drinks, deck chairs etc. could be stored.

# Using our Garden

The hospital auxiliary had asked us to host the annual fete, we felt the garden was now established enough to be suitable and the wide slate verandas would accommodate stalls if the weather was inclement. So, we were happy to do so.

The day came and it was a beautiful sunny day. The helpers came early, and the various stalls were set up on the lawn. Handicraft, cake and biscuits, garden produce, cuttings and plants, jumble, miscellaneous and most importantly a strawberry and ice-cream stall. People began arriving, it was certainly going to be a large gathering. Scones, jam & cream, tea and coffee, which Becky and I had made were available for a gold coin donation. The stall holders were kept very busy. It was a great financial success as well as an enjoyable social outing for those attending. Tired but happy with the success of the day Blake and I with Gordon and Becky did a tidy up and emptied bins and the garden looked almost as usual again.

After the hospital fete we were asked by our neighbours daughter if she could have her wedding in our garden. We were happy for this to happen. It gave me an idea. There was a beautiful gum tree just to the side of the main garden and we had discovered a crazy slate stone path leading down to it. Our gardener had watered there, and bulbs were popping up, hyacinths, jonquils and freesias, the flowers issuing such sweet smells., I hoped some daffodils would come up too and add their brilliant yellow among the others as they flowered. All we needed was to add a wrought iron archway and some ferns and greenery, and what a delightful spot this would be for the actual ceremony. The wedding day came, and it all went very smoothly. The couple had some photos taken, then mingled with their guests on the spacious lawns and enjoyed nibbles and champagne which they had provided before departing for their reception in the local hall.

Soon we were receiving more requests from young couples to have their ceremony in our garden. It gave me an idea we could offer a Marriage celebrant. I ran this idea by Becky and Gordon, Becky thought it would be wonderful and was prepared to do the necessary study to become a licensed celebrant. We could offer this when asked for the use of the garden, whether they accepted this or not was up to them.

Our garden became a regular venue for weddings, we also enjoyed the happiness it brought to the young couple. As they appreciated the natural beauty of the garden.

There was no charge for the use of the garden, the couple could make a donation to the Hospital Auxiliary if they felt obligated.

There were horse stables which Blake and I discovered on one of our walks. Blakes Haven must have been a wonderful station in its' time before being subdivided into smaller holdings.

The stables could be converted into a reception room and a kitchen added for caterers. My brain was in overdrive with possibilities.

Blake had other ideas. He reminded me that we were retired and had another holiday planned cruising the Pacific Islands and having a week on Tahiti, before cruising around New Zealand and going ashore whenever possible.

Blake also reminded me, he wanted to establish an "Australian White" sheep stud when we returned from our Pacific islands cruise. He wanted the stables to store sheep requisites. I wasn't opposed to the idea of an Australian White sheep stud as Blake was very interested in the stud on my home farm at Angaston. Australian White sheep are a low maintenance breed, and it would be great to see lambs frolicking in the paddocks, and maybe I'd have a pet lamb.

All our plans gave us plenty to think and talk about, so much so we spent a lot of time on computers and in the study, Freddie was very happy to have a bit more company than usual. We often talked long into the night until we fell asleep.

# Relaxing

We were now self-sufficient with our vegetables and fruit from the orchard. We always enjoyed a stroll down to the river, there were more water birds coming into the wetlands as the new grasses Blake had planted were now well established. Plovers, duck's mallee fowls, herons, galahs others that I didn't know. Blake liked to dangle his fishing line in from his old tinnie, occasionally he would catch a carp.

I liked to read, or paint, the scenery with so many beautiful trees and grasses of all colours and the reflections on the river, the sunsets, the pelicans, and ducks all so graceful occasionally a Kookaburra all made good subjects and added to the scenic beauty. I now stored my paints and canvases in the boat shed so much easier than carrying them down from the house. This was such a peaceful tranquil place to be.

Blake often reminded me that we were now retired and so maybe we should think about slowing down. We still planned to visit Birdsville, Alice Springs, Uluru and the gorges, Australia has so much to offer, we could choose where and when to fit in with our local commitments.

# On the Road

We were so happy just being together and loved being home at Blakes Haven where we could enjoy our life together as best friends and passionate lovers. However, we needed go around Australia as we had planned to do this before we were too old and explore more than just each other.

We decided to travel to Darwin on the Gahn, buy a Motor Home there and then travel back through Kununurra and Fitzroy Crossing, cruise the Geike Gorge then on to Broome (a camel ride along Cable Beach was a highlight) and down the west coast, Karratha, Exmouth a stop over to feed the dolphins at Monkey Mia, continue along the coast and see Claudia and Jordan Davey with whom we kept in touch and were now settled into their retirement home at Cottesloe. We spent two days with them, and we all decided to travel down to Albany and spend a few days, whilst there we also went out to Rottnest Island on a hovercraft. We were bussed around the island and even saw a quokka. We said our goodbyes and Claudia and Jordan left to return to Cottesloe and we to go to Norsman and travel home across the Nullarbor Plain. At the Great Australian Bight we did some whale watching. We were so lucky to see several whales, their black and white bodies so visible in the clear water, a calf at play delighted us by jumping up and down in and out of the water. On the home-ward stretch now and keen to get there. The families at Angaston wanted us to call there on our way home. It was so good to see them all but even better to arrive home at Blakes Haven. In the future short visits to Angaston and to Melbourne for special occasions would of course always be on our agenda. Life was indeed wonderful as we shared our sunset years truly in bliss and deep love for one another.

*The End*